THE PURSE

By Honore De Balzac

THE PURSE

For souls to whom effusiveness is easy there is a delicious hour that falls when it is not yet night, but is no longer day; the twilight gleam throws softened lights or tricksy reflections on every object, and favors a dreamy mood which vaguely weds itself to the play of light and shade. The silence which generally prevails at that time makes it particularly dear to artists, who grow contemplative, stand a few paces back from the pictures on which they can no longer work, and pass judgement on them, rapt by the subject whose most recondite meaning then flashes on the inner eye of genius. He who has never stood pensive by a friend's side in such an hour of poetic dreaming can hardly understand its inexpressible soothingness. Favored by the clear-obscure, the material skill employed by art to produce illusion entirely disappears. If the work is a picture, the figures represented seem to speak and walk; the shade is shadow, the light is day; the flesh lives, eyes move, blood flows in their veins, and stuffs have a changing sheen. Imagination helps the realism of every detail, and only sees the beauties of the work. At that hour illusion reigns despotically; perhaps it wakes at nightfall! Is not illusion a sort of night to the mind, which we people with dreams? Illusion then unfolds its wings, it bears the soul aloft to the world of fancies, a world full of voluptuous imaginings, where the artist forgets the real world, yesterday and the morrow, the future — everything down to its miseries, the good and the evil alike.

At this magic hour a young painter, a man of talent, who saw in art nothing but Art itself, was perched on a step-ladder which helped him to work at a large high painting, now nearly finished. Criticising himself, honestly admiring himself, floating on the current of his thoughts, he then lost himself in one of those meditative moods which ravish and elevate the soul, soothe it, and comfort it. His reverie had no doubt lasted a long time. Night fell. Whether he meant to come down from his perch, or whether he made some ill-judged movement, believing himself to be on the floor — the event did not allow of his remembering exactly the cause of his accident — he fell, his head struck a footstool, he lost consciousness and lay motionless during a space of time of which he knew not the length.

A sweet voice roused him from the stunned condition into which he had sunk. When he opened his eyes the flash of a bright light made him close them again immediately; but through the mist that veiled his senses he heard the whispering of two women, and felt two young, two timid hands on which his head was resting. He soon recovered consciousness, and by the light of an old-fashioned Argand lamp he could make out the most charming girl's face he had ever seen, one of those heads which are often supposed to be a freak of the brush, but which to him suddenly realized the theories of the ideal beauty which every artist creates for himself and whence his art proceeds. The features of the unknown belonged, so to say, to the refined and delicate type of Prudhon's school, but had also the poetic sentiment which Girodet gave to the inventions of his phantasy. The freshness of the temples, the regular arch of the eyebrows, the purity of outline, the virginal innocence so plainly stamped on every feature of her countenance, made the girl a perfect creature. Her figure was slight and graceful, and frail in form. Her dress, though simple and neat, revealed neither wealth nor penury.

As he recovered his senses, the painter gave expression to his admiration by a look of surprise, and stammered some confused thanks. He found a handkerchief pressed to his forehead, and above the smell peculiar to a studio, he recognized the strong odor of ether, applied no doubt to revive him from his fainting fit. Finally he saw an old woman, looking like a marquise of the old school, who held the lamp and was advising the young girl.

"Monsieur," said the younger woman in reply to one of the questions put by the painter during the few minutes when he was still under the influence of the vagueness that the shock had produced in his ideas, "my mother and I heard the noise of your fall on the floor, and we fancied we heard a groan. The silence following on the crash alarmed us, and we hurried up. Finding the key in the latch, we happily took the liberty of entering, and we found you lying motionless on the ground. My mother went to fetch what was needed to bathe your head and revive you. You have cut your forehead — there. Do you feel it?"

"Yes, I do now," he replied.

"Oh, it will be nothing," said the old mother. "Happily your head rested against this lay-figure."

"I feel infinitely better," replied the painter. "I need nothing further but a hackney cab to take me home. The porter's wife will go for one."

He tried to repeat his thanks to the two strangers; but at each sentence the elder lady interrupted him, saying, "Tomorrow, monsieur, pray be careful to put on leeches, or to be bled, and drink a few cups of something healing. A fall may be dangerous."

The young girl stole a look at the painter and at the pictures in the studio. Her expression and her glances revealed perfect propriety; her curiosity seemed rather absence of mind, and her eyes seemed to speak the interest which women feel, with the most engaging spontaneity, in everything which causes us suffering. The two strangers seemed to forget the painter's works in the painter's mishap. When he had reassured them as to his condition they left, looking at him with an anxiety that was equally free from insistence and from familiarity, without asking any indiscreet questions, or trying to incite him to any wish to visit them. Their proceedings all bore the hall-mark of natural refinement and good taste. Their noble and simple manners at first made no great impression on the painter, but subsequently, as he recalled all the details of the incident, he was greatly struck by them.

When they reached the floor beneath that occupied by the painter's studio, the old lady gently observed, "Adelaide, you left the door open."

"That was to come to my assistance," said the painter, with a grateful smile.

"You came down just now, mother," replied the young girl, with a blush.

"Would you like us to accompany you all the way downstairs?" asked the mother. "The stairs are dark."

"No, thank you, indeed, madame; I am much better."

"Hold tightly by the rail."

The two women remained on the landing to light the young man, listening to the sound of his steps.

In order to set forth clearly all the exciting and unexpected interest this scene might have for the young painter, it must be told that he had only a few days since established his studio in the attics of this house, situated in the darkest and, therefore, the most muddy part of the Rue de Suresnes, almost opposite the Church of the Madeleine, and quite close to his rooms in the Rue des Champs-Elysees. The fame his talent had won him having made him one of the artists most dear to his country, he was beginning to feel free from want, and to use his own expression, was enjoying his last privations. Instead of going to his work in one of the studios near the city gates, where the moderate rents had hitherto been in proportion to his humble earnings, he had gratified a wish that was new every morning, by sparing himself a long walk, and the loss of much time, now more valuable than ever.

No man in the world would have inspired feelings of greater interest than Hippolyte Schinner if he would ever have consented to make acquaintance; but he did not lightly entrust to others the secrets of his life. He was the idol of a necessitous mother, who had brought him up at the cost of the severest privations. Mademoiselle Schinner, the daughter of an Alsatian farmer, had never been married. Her tender soul had been cruelly crushed, long ago, by a rich man, who did not pride himself on any great delicacy in his love affairs. The day when, as a young girl, in all the radiance of her beauty and all the triumph of her life, she suffered, at the cost of her heart and her sweet illusions, the disenchantment which falls on us so slowly and yet so quickly—for we try to postpone as long as possible our belief in evil, and it seems to come too soon—that day was a whole age of reflection, and it was also a day of religious thought and resignation. She refused the alms of the man who had betrayed her, renounced the world, and made a glory of her shame. She gave herself up entirely to her motherly love, seeking in it all her joys in exchange for the social pleasures to which she bid farewell. She lived by work, saving up a treasure for her son. And, in after years, a day, an hour repaid her amply for the long and weary sacrifices of her indigence.

At the last exhibition her son had received the Cross of the Legion of Honor. The newspapers, unanimous in hailing an unknown genius, still rang with sincere praises. Artists themselves acknowledged Schinner as a master, and dealers covered his canvases with gold pieces. At five-and-twenty Hippolyte Schinner, to whom his mother had transmitted her woman's soul, understood more clearly than ever his position in the world. Anxious to restore to his mother the pleasures of which society had so long robbed her, he lived for her, hoping by the aid of fame and fortune to see her one day happy, rich, respected, and surrounded by men of mark. Schinner had therefore chosen his friends among the most honorable and distinguished men. Fastidious in the selection of his intimates, he desired to raise still further a position which his talent had placed high. The work to which he had devoted himself from boyhood, by compelling him to dwell in solitude—the mother of great thoughts—had left him the beautiful beliefs which grace the early days of life. His adolescent soul was not closed to any of the thousand bashful emotions by which a young man is a being apart, whose heart abounds in joys, in poetry, in virginal hopes, puerile in the eyes of men of the world, but deep because they are single-hearted.

He was endowed with the gentle and polite manners which speak to the soul, and fascinate even those who do not understand them. He was well made. His voice, coming from his heart, stirred that of others to noble sentiments, and bore witness to his true modesty by a certain ingenuousness of tone. Those who saw him felt drawn to him by that attraction of the moral nature which men of science are happily unable to analyze; they would detect in it some phenomenon of galvanism, or the current of I know not what fluid, and express our sentiments in a formula of ratios of oxygen and electricity.

These details will perhaps explain to strong-minded persons and to men of fashion why, in the absence of the porter whom he had sent to the end of the Rue de la Madeleine to call him a coach, Hippolyte Schinner did not ask the man's wife any questions concerning the two women whose kindness of heart had shown itself in his behalf. But though he replied Yes or No to the inquiries, natural under the circumstances, which the good woman made as to his accident, and the friendly intervention of the tenants occupying the fourth floor, he could not hinder her from following the instinct of her kind; she mentioned the two strangers, speaking of them as prompted by the interests of her policy and the subterranean opinions of the porter's lodge.

"Ah," said she, "they were, no doubt, Mademoiselle Leseigneur and her mother, who have lived here these four years. We do not know exactly what these ladies do; in the morning, only till the hour of noon, an old woman who is half deaf, and who never speaks any more than a wall, comes in to help them; in the evening, two or three old gentlemen, with loops of ribbon, like you, monsieur, come to see them, and often stay very late. One of them comes in a carriage with servants, and is said to have sixty thousand francs a year. However, they are very quiet tenants, as you are, monsieur; and economical! they live on nothing, and as soon as a letter is brought they pay for it. It is a queer thing, monsieur, the mother's name is not the same as the daughter's. Ah, but when they go for a walk in the Tuileries, mademoiselle is very smart, and she never goes out but she is followed by a lot of young men; but she shuts the door in their face, and she is quite right. The proprietor would never allow — — "

The coach having come, Hippolyte heard no more, and went home. His mother, to whom he related his adventure, dressed his wound afresh, and would not allow him to go to the studio next day. After taking advice, various treatments were prescribed, and Hippolyte remained at home three days. During this retirement his idle fancy recalled vividly, bit by bit, the details of the scene that had ensued on his fainting fit. The young girl's profile was clearly projected against the darkness of his inward vision; he saw once more the mother's faded features, or he felt the touch of Adelaide's hands. He remembered some gesture which at first had not greatly struck him, but whose exquisite grace was thrown into relief by memory; then an attitude, or the tones of a melodious voice, enhanced by the distance of remembrance, suddenly rose before him, as objects plunging to the bottom of deep waters come back to the surface.

So, on the day when he could resume work, he went early to his studio; but the visit he undoubtedly had a right to pay to his neighbors was the true cause of his haste; he had already forgotten the pictures he had begun. At the moment when a passion throws off its swaddling clothes, inexplicable pleasures are felt, known to those who have loved. So some readers will understand why the painter mounted the stairs to the fourth floor but slowly, and will be in the secret of the throbs that followed each other so rapidly in his heart at the moment when he saw the humble brown door of the rooms inhabited by Mademoiselle Leseigneur. This girl, whose name was not the same as her mother's, had aroused the young painter's deepest sympathies; he chose to fancy some similarity between himself and her as to their position, and attributed to her misfortunes of birth akin to his own. All the time he worked Hippolyte gave himself very willingly to thoughts of love, and made a great deal of noise to compel the two ladies to think of him, as he was thinking of them. He stayed late at the studio and dined there; then, at about seven o'clock, he went down to call on his neighbors.

No painter of manners has ventured to initiate us — perhaps out of modesty — into the really curious privacy of certain Parisian existences, into the secret of the dwellings whence emerge such fresh and elegant toilets, such brilliant women, who rich on the surface, allow the signs of very doubtful comfort to peep out in every part of their home. If, here, the picture is too boldly drawn, if you find it tedious in places, do not blame the description, which is, indeed, part and parcel of my story; for the appearance of the rooms inhabited by his two neighbors had a great influence on the feelings and hopes of Hippolyte Schinner.

The house belonged to one of those proprietors in whom there is a foregone and profound horror of repairs and decoration, one of the men who regard their position as Paris house-owners as a business. In the vast chain of moral species, these people hold a middle place between the miser and the usurer. Optimists in their own interests, they are all faithful to the Austrian status quo. If you speak of moving a cupboard or a door, of opening the most indispensable air-hole, their eyes flash, their bile rises, they rear like a frightened horse. When the wind blows down a few chimney-pots they are quite ill, and deprive themselves of an evening at the Gymnase or the Porte-Saint-Martin Theatre, "on account of repairs." Hippolyte, who had seen the performance gratis of a comical scene with Monsieur Molineux as concerning certain decorative repairs in his studio, was not surprised to see the dark greasy paint, the oily stains, spots, and other disagreeable accessories that varied the woodwork. And these stigmata of poverty are not altogether devoid of poetry in an artist's eyes.

Mademoiselle Leseigneur herself opened the door. On recognizing the young artist she bowed, and at the same time, with Parisian adroitness, and with the presence of mind that pride can lend, she turned round to shut the door in a glass partition through which Hippolyte might have caught sight of some linen hung by lines over patent ironing stoves, an old camp-bed, some wood-embers, charcoal, irons, a filter, the household crockery, and all the utensils familiar to a small household. Muslin curtains, fairly white, carefully screened this lumber-room — a *capharnaum*, as the French call such a domestic laboratory, — which was lighted by windows looking out on a neighboring yard.

Hippolyte, with the quick eye of an artist, saw the uses, the furniture, the general effect and condition of this first room, thus cut in half. The more honorable half, which served both as ante-room and dining-room, was hung with an old salmon-rose-colored paper, with a flock border, the manufacture of Reveillon, no doubt; the holes and spots had been carefully touched over with wafers. Prints representing the battles of Alexander, by Lebrun, in frames with the gilding rubbed off were symmetrically arranged on the walls. In the middle stood a massive mahogany table, old-fashioned in shape, and worn at the edges. A small stove, whose thin straight pipe was scarcely visible, stood in front of the chimney-place, but the hearth was occupied by a cupboard. By a strange contrast the chairs showed some remains of former splendor; they were of carved mahogany, but the red morocco seats, the gilt nails and reeded backs, showed as many scars as an old sergeant of the Imperial Guard.

This room did duty as a museum of certain objects, such as are never seen but in this kind of amphibious household; nameless objects with the stamp at once of luxury and penury. Among other curiosities Hippolyte noticed a splendidly finished telescope, hanging over the small discolored glass that decorated the chimney. To harmonize with this strange collection of furniture, there was, between the chimney and the partition, a wretched sideboard of painted wood, pretending to be mahogany, of all woods the most impossible to imitate. But the slippery red quarries, the shabby little rugs in front of the chairs, and all the furniture, shone with the hard rubbing cleanliness which lends a treacherous lustre to old things by making their defects, their age, and their long service still more conspicuous. An indescribable odor pervaded the room, a mingled smell of the exhalations from the lumber room, and the vapors of the dining-room, with those from the stairs, though the window was partly open. The air from the street fluttered the dusty curtains, which were carefully drawn so as to hide the window bay, where former tenants had testified to their presence by various ornamental additions — a sort of domestic fresco.

Adelaide hastened to open the door of the inner room, where she announced the painter with evident pleasure. Hippolyte, who, of yore, had seen the same signs of poverty in his mother's home, noted them with the singular vividness of impression which characterizes the earliest acquisitions of memory, and entered into the details of this existence better than any one else would have done. As he recognized the facts of his life as a child, the kind young fellow felt neither scorn for disguised misfortune nor pride in the luxury he had lately conquered for his mother.

"Well, monsieur, I hope you no longer feel the effects of your fall," said the old lady, rising from an antique armchair that stood by the chimney, and offering him a seat.

"No, madame. I have come to thank you for the kind care you gave me, and above all mademoiselle, who heard me fall."

As he uttered this speech, stamped with the exquisite stupidity given to the mind by the first disturbing symptoms of true love, Hippolyte looked at the young girl. Adelaide was lighting the Argand lamp, no doubt that she might get rid of a tallow candle fixed in a large copper flat candlestick, and graced with a heavy fluting of grease from its guttering. She answered with a slight bow, carried the flat candlestick into the ante-room, came back, and after placing the lamp on the chimney shelf, seated herself by her mother, a little behind the painter, so as to be able to look at him at her ease, while apparently much interested in the burning of the lamp; the flame, checked by the damp in a dingy chimney, sputtered as it struggled with a charred and badly-trimmed wick. Hippolyte, seeing the large mirror that decorated the chimney-piece, immediately fixed his eyes on it to admire Adelaide. Thus the girl's little stratagem only served to embarrass them both.

While talking with Madame Leseigneur, for Hippolyte called her so, on the chance of being right, he examined the room, but unobtrusively and by stealth.

The Egyptian figures on the iron fire-dogs were scarcely visible, the hearth was so heaped with cinders; two brands tried to meet in front of a sham log of fire-brick, as carefully buried as a miser's treasure could ever be. An old Aubusson carpet, very much faded, very much mended, and as worn as a pensioner's coat, did not cover the whole of the tiled floor, and the cold struck to his feet. The walls were hung with a reddish paper, imitating figured silk with a yellow pattern. In the middle of the wall opposite the windows the painter saw a crack, and the outline marked on the paper of double-doors, shutting off a recess where Madame Leseigneur slept no doubt, a fact ill disguised by a sofa in front of the door. Facing the chimney, above a mahogany chest of drawers of handsome and tasteful design, was the portrait of an officer of rank, which the dim light did not allow him to see well; but from what he could make out he thought that the fearful daub must have been painted in China. The window-curtains of red silk were as much faded as the furniture, in red and yellow worsted work, [as] if this room "contrived a double debt to pay." On the marble top of the chest of drawers was a costly malachite tray, with a dozen coffee cups magnificently painted and made, no doubt, at Sevres. On the chimney shelf stood the omnipresent Empire clock: a warrior driving the four horses of a chariot, whose wheel bore the numbers of the hours on its spokes. The tapers in the tall candlesticks were yellow with smoke, and at each corner of the shelf stood a porcelain vase crowned with artificial flowers full of dust and stuck into moss.

In the middle of the room Hippolyte remarked a card-table ready for play, with new packs of cards. For an observer there was something heartrending in the sight of this misery painted up like an old woman who wants to falsify her face. At such a sight every man of sense must at once have stated to himself this obvious dilemma — either these two women are honesty itself, or they live by intrigue and gambling. But on looking at Adelaide, a man so pure-minded as Schinner could not but believe in her perfect innocence, and ascribe the incoherence of the furniture to honorable causes.

"My dear," said the old lady to the young one, "I am cold; make a little fire, and give me my shawl."

Adelaide went into a room next the drawing-room, where she no doubt slept, and returned bringing her mother a cashmere shawl, which when new must have been very costly; the pattern was Indian; but it was old, faded and full of darns, and matched the furniture. Madame Leseigneur wrapped herself in it very artistically, and with the readiness of an old woman who wishes to make her words seem truth. The young girl ran lightly off to the lumber-room and reappeared with a bundle of small wood, which she gallantly threw on the fire to revive it.

It would be rather difficult to reproduce the conversation which followed among these three persons. Hippolyte, guided by the tact which is almost always the outcome of misfortune suffered in early youth, dared not allow himself to make the least remark as to his neighbors' situation, as he saw all about him the signs of ill-disguised poverty. The simplest question would have been an indiscretion, and could only be ventured on by old friendship. The painter was nevertheless absorbed in the thought of this concealed penury, it pained his generous soul; but knowing how offensive every kind of pity may be, even the friendliest, the disparity between his thoughts and his words made him feel uncomfortable.

The two ladies at first talked of painting, for women easily guess the secret embarrassment of a first call; they themselves feel it perhaps, and the nature of their mind supplies them with a thousand devices to put an end to it. By questioning the young man as to the material exercise of his art, and as to his studies, Adelaide and her mother emboldened him to talk. The indefinable nothings of their chat, animated by kind feeling, naturally led Hippolyte to flash forth remarks or reflections which showed the character of his habits and of his mind. Trouble had prematurely faded the old lady's face, formerly handsome, no doubt; nothing was left but the more prominent features, the outline, in a word, the skeleton of a countenance of which the whole effect indicated great shrewdness with much grace in the play of the eyes, in which could be discerned the expression peculiar to women of the old Court; an expression that cannot be defined in words. Those fine and mobile features might quite as well indicate bad feelings, and suggest astuteness and womanly artifice carried to a high pitch of wickedness, as reveal the refined delicacy of a beautiful soul.

Indeed, the face of a woman has this element of mystery to puzzle the ordinary observer, that the difference between frankness and duplicity, the genius for intrigue and the genius of the heart, is there inscrutable. A man gifted with the penetrating eye can read the intangible shade of difference produced by a more or less curved line, a more or less deep dimple, a more or less prominent feature. The appreciation of these indications lies entirely in the domain of intuition; this alone can lead to the discovery of what everyone is interested in concealing. The old lady's face was like the room she inhabited; it seemed as difficult to detect whether this squalor covered vice or the highest virtue, as to decide whether Adelaide's mother was an old coquette accustomed to weigh, to calculate, to sell everything, or a loving woman, full of noble feeling and amiable qualities. But at Schinner's age the first impulse of the heart is to believe in goodness. And indeed, as he studied Adelaide's noble and almost haughty brow, as he looked into her eyes full of soul and thought, he breathed, so to speak, the sweet and modest fragrance of virtue. In the course of the conversation he seized an opportunity of discussing portraits in general, to give himself a pretext for examining the frightful *pastel*, of which the color had flown, and the chalk in many places fallen away.

"You are attached to that picture for the sake of the likeness, no doubt, mesdames, for the drawing is dreadful?" he said, looking at Adelaide.

"It was done at Calcutta, in great haste," replied the mother in an agitated voice.

She gazed at the formless sketch with the deep absorption which memories of happiness produce when they are roused and fall on the heart like a beneficent dew to whose refreshing touch we love to yield ourselves up; but in the expression of the old lady's face there were traces too of perennial regret. At least, it was thus that the painter chose to interpret her attitude and countenance, and he presently sat down again by her side.

"Madame," he said, "in a very short time the colors of that pastel will have disappeared. The portrait will only survive in your memory. Where you will still see the face that is dear to you, others will see nothing at all. Will you allow me to reproduce the likeness on canvas? It will be more permanently recorded then than on that sheet of paper. Grant me, I beg, as a neighborly favor, the pleasure of doing you this service. There are times when an artist is glad of a respite from his greater undertakings by doing work of less lofty pretensions, so it will be a recreation for me to paint that head."

The old lady flushed as she heard the painter's words, and Adelaide shot one of those glances of deep feeling which seem to flash from the soul. Hippolyte wanted to feel some tie linking him with his two neighbors, to conquer a right to mingle in their life. His offer, appealing as it did to the liveliest affections of the heart, was the only one he could possibly make; it gratified his pride as an artist, and could not hurt the feelings of the ladies. Madame Leseigneur accepted, without eagerness or reluctance, but with the self-possession of a noble soul, fully aware of the character of bonds formed by such an obligation, while, at the same time, they are its highest glory as a proof of esteem.

"I fancy," said the painter, "that the uniform is that of a naval officer."

"Yes," she said, "that of a captain in command of a vessel. Monsieur de Rouville—my husband—died at Batavia in consequence of a wound received in a fight with an English ship they fell in with off the Asiatic coast. He commanded a frigate of fifty-six guns and the *Revenge* carried ninety-six. The struggle was very unequal, but he defended his ship so bravely that he held out till nightfall and got away. When I came back to France Bonaparte was not yet in power, and I was refused a pension. When I applied again for it, quite lately, I was sternly informed that if the Baron de Rouville had emigrated I should not have lost him; that by this time he would have been a rear-admiral; finally, his Excellency quoted I know not what degree of forfeiture. I took this step, to which I was urged by my friends, only for the sake of my poor Adelaide. I have always hated the idea of holding out my hand as a beggar in the name of a grief which deprives a woman of voice and strength. I do not like this money valuation for blood irreparably spilt — — "

"Dear mother, this subject always does you harm."

In response to this remark from Adelaide, the Baronne Leseigneur bowed, and was silent.

"Monsieur," said the young girl to Hippolyte, "I had supposed that a painter's work was generally fairly quiet?"

At this question Schinner colored, remembering the noise he had made. Adelaide said no more, and spared him a falsehood by rising at the sound of a carriage stopping at the door. She went into her own room, and returned carrying a pair of tall gilt candlesticks with partly burnt wax candles, which she quickly lighted, and without waiting for the bell to ring, she opened the door of the outer room, where she set the lamp down. The sound of a kiss given and received found an echo in Hippolyte's heart. The young man's impatience to see the man who treated Adelaide with so much familiarity was not immediately gratified; the newcomers had a conversation, which he thought very long, in an undertone, with the young girl.

At last Mademoiselle de Rouville returned, followed by two men, whose costume, countenance, and appearance are a long story.

The first, a man of about sixty, wore one of the coats invented, I believe, for Louis XVIII., then on the throne, in which the most difficult problem of the sartorial art had been solved by a tailor who ought to be immortal. That artist certainly understood the art of compromise, which was the moving genius of that period of shifting politics. Is it not a rare merit to be able to take the measure of the time? This coat, which the young men of the present day may conceive to be fabulous, was neither civil nor military, and might pass for civil or military by turns. Fleurs-de-lis were embroidered on the lapels of the back skirts. The gilt buttons also bore fleurs-de-lis; on the shoulders a pair of straps cried out for useless epaulettes; these military appendages were there like a petition without a recommendation. This old gentleman's coat was of dark blue cloth, and the buttonhole had blossomed into many colored ribbons. He, no doubt, always carried his hat in his hand—a three cornered cocked hat, with a gold cord—for the snowy wings of his powdered hair showed not a trace of its pressure. He might have been taken for not more than fifty years of age, and seemed to enjoy robust health. While wearing the frank and loyal expression of the old emigres, his countenance also hinted at the easy habits of a libertine, at the light and reckless passions of the Musketeers formerly so famous in the annals of gallantry. His gestures, his attitude, and his manner proclaimed that he had no intention of correcting himself of his royalism, of his religion, or of his love affairs.

A really fantastic figure came in behind this specimen of "Louis XIV.'s light infantry"—a nickname given by the Bonapartists to these venerable survivors of the Monarchy. To do it justice it ought to be made the principal object in the picture, and it is but an accessory. Imagine a lean, dry man, dressed like the former, but seeming to be only his reflection, or his shadow, if you will. The coat, new on the first, on the second was old; the powder in his hair looked less white, the gold of the fleurs-de-lis less bright, the shoulder straps more hopeless and dog's eared; his intellect seemed more feeble, his life nearer the fatal term than in the former. In short, he realized Rivarol's witticism on Champcenetz, "He is the moonlight of me." He was simply his double, a paler and poorer double, for there was between them all the difference that lies between the first and last impressions of a lithograph.

This speechless old man was a mystery to the painter, and always remained a mystery. The Chevalier, for he was a Chevalier, did not speak, nobody spoke to him. Was he a friend, a poor relation, a man who followed at the old gallant's heels as a lady companion does at an old lady's? Did he fill a place midway between a dog, a parrot, and a friend? Had he saved his patron's fortune, or only his life? Was he the Trim to another Captain Toby? Elsewhere, as at the Baronne de Rouville's, he always piqued curiosity without satisfying it. Who, after the Restoration, could remember the attachment which, before the Revolution, had bound this man to his friend's wife, dead now these twenty year?

The leader, who appeared the least dilapidated of these wrecks, came gallantly up to Madame de Rouville, kissed her hand, and sat down by her. The other bowed and placed himself not far from his model, at a distance represented by two chairs. Adelaide came behind the old gentleman's armchair and leaned her elbows on the back, unconsciously imitating the attitude given to Dido's sister by Guerin in his famous picture.

Though the gentleman's familiarity was that of a father, his freedom seemed at the moment to annoy the young girl.

"What, are you sulky with me?" he said.

Then he shot at Schinner one of those side-looks full of shrewdness and cunning, diplomatic looks, whose expression betrays the discreet uneasiness, the polite curiosity of well-bred people, and seems to ask, when they see a stranger, "Is he one of us?"

"This is our neighbor," said the old lady, pointing to Hippolyte. "Monsieur is a celebrated painter, whose name must be known to you in spite of your indifference to the arts."

The old man saw his friend's mischievous intent in suppressing the name, and bowed to the young man.

"Certainly," said he. "I heard a great deal about his pictures at the last Salon. Talent has immense privileges." he added, observing the artist's red ribbon. "That distinction, which we must earn at the cost of our blood and long service, you win in your youth; but all glory is of the same kindred," he said, laying his hand on his Cross of Saint-Louis.

Hippolyte murmured a few words of acknowledgment, and was silent again, satisfied to admire with growing enthusiasm the beautiful girl's head that charmed him so much. He was soon lost in contemplation, completely forgetting the extreme misery of the dwelling. To him Adelaide's face stood out against a luminous atmosphere. He replied briefly to the questions addressed to him, which, by good luck, he heard, thanks to a singular faculty of the soul which sometimes seems to have a double consciousness. Who has not known what it is to sit lost in sad or delicious meditation, listening to its voice within, while attending to a conversation or to reading? An admirable duality which often helps us to tolerate a bore! Hope, prolific and smiling, poured out before him a thousand visions of happiness; and he refused to consider what was going on around him. As confiding as a child, it seemed to him base to analyze a pleasure.

After a short lapse of time he perceived that the old lady and her daughter were playing cards with the old gentleman. As to the satellite, faithful to his function as a shadow, he stood behind his friend's chair watching his game, and answering the player's mute inquiries by little approving nods, repeating the questioning gestures of the other countenance.

"Du Halga, I always lose," said the gentleman.

"You discard badly," replied the Baronne de Rouville.

"For three months now I have never won a single game," said he.

"Have you the aces?" asked the old lady.

"Yes, one more to mark," said he.

"Shall I come and advise you?" said Adelaide.

"No, no. Stay where I can see you. By Gad, it would be losing too much not to have you to look at!"

At last the game was over. The gentleman pulled out his purse, and, throwing two louis d'or on the table, not without temper —

"Forty francs," he exclaimed, "the exact sum. — Deuce take it! It is eleven o'clock."

"It is eleven o'clock," repeated the silent figure, looking at the painter.

The young man, hearing these words rather more distinctly than all the others, thought it time to retire. Coming back to the world of ordinary ideas, he found a few commonplace remarks to make, took leave of the Baroness, her daughter, and the two strangers, and went away, wholly possessed by the first raptures of true love, without attempting to analyze the little incidents of the evening.

On the morrow the young painter felt the most ardent desire to see Adelaide once more. If he had followed the call of his passion, he would have gone to his neighbor's door at six in the morning, when he went to his studio. However, he still was reasonable enough to wait till the afternoon. But as soon as he thought he could present himself to Madame de Rouville, he went downstairs, rang, blushing like a girl, shyly asked Mademoiselle Leseigneur, who came to let him in, to let him have the portrait of the Baron.

"But come in," said Adelaide, who had no doubt heard him come down from the studio.

The painter followed, bashful and out of countenance, not knowing what to say, happiness had so dulled his wit. To see Adelaide, to hear the rustle of her skirt, after longing for a whole morning to be near her, after starting up a hundred time — "I will go down now" — and not to have gone; this was to him life so rich that such sensations, too greatly prolonged, would have worn out his spirit. The heart has the singular power of giving extraordinary value to mere nothings. What joy it is to a traveler to treasure a blade of grass, an unfamiliar leaf, if he has risked his life to pluck it! It is the same with the trifles of love.

The old lady was not in the drawing-room. When the young girl found herself there, alone with the painter, she brought a chair to stand on, to take down the picture; but perceiving that she could not unhook it without setting her foot on the chest of drawers, she turned to Hippolyte, and said with a blush:

"I am not tall enough. Will you get it down?"

A feeling of modesty, betrayed in the expression of her face and the tones of her voice, was the real motive of her request; and the young man, understanding this, gave her one of those glances of intelligence which are the sweetest language of love. Seeing that the painter had read her soul, Adelaide cast down her eyes with the instinct of reserve which is the secret of a maiden's heart. Hippolyte, finding nothing to say, and feeling almost timid, took down the picture, examined it gravely, carrying it to the light of the window, and then went away, without saying a word to Mademoiselle Leseigneur but, "I will return it soon."

During this brief moment they both went through one of those storms of agitation of which the effects in the soul may be compared to those of a stone flung into a deep lake. The most delightful waves of thought rise and follow each other, indescribable, repeated, and aimless, tossing the heart like the circular ripples, which for a long time fret the waters, starting from the point where the stone fell.

Hippolyte returned to the studio bearing the portrait. His easel was ready with a fresh canvas, and his palette set, his brushes cleaned, the spot and the light carefully chosen. And till the dinner hour he worked at the painting with the ardor artists throw into their whims. He went again that evening to the Baronne de Rouville's, and remained from nine till eleven. Excepting the different topics of conversation, this evening was exactly like the last. The two old men arrived at the same hour, the same game of piquet was played, the same speeches made by the players, the sum lost by Adelaide's friend was not less considerable than on the previous evening; only Hippolyte, a little bolder, ventured to chat with the young girl.

A week passed thus, and in the course of it the painter's feelings and Adelaide's underwent the slow and delightful transformations which bring two souls to a perfect understanding. Every day the look with which the girl welcomed her friend grew more intimate, more confiding, gayer, and more open; her voice and manner became more eager and more familiar. They laughed and talked together, telling each other their thoughts, speaking of themselves with the simplicity of two children who have made friends in a day, as much as if they had met constantly for three years. Schinner wished to be taught piquet. Being ignorant and a novice, he, of course, made blunder after blunder, and like the old man, he lost almost every game. Without having spoken a word of love the lovers knew that they were all in all to one another. Hippolyte enjoyed exerting his power over his gentle little friend, and many concessions were made to him by Adelaide, who, timid and devoted to him, was quite deceived by the assumed fits of temper, such as the least skilled lover and the most guileless girl can affect; and which they constantly play off, as spoilt children abuse the power they owe to their mother's affection. Thus all familiarity between the girl and the old Count was soon put a stop to. She understood the painter's melancholy, and the thoughts hidden in the furrows on his brow, from the abrupt tone of the few words he spoke when the old man unceremoniously kissed Adelaide's hands or throat.

Mademoiselle Leseigneur, on her part, soon expected her lover to give a short account of all his actions; she was so unhappy, so restless when Hippolyte did not come, she scolded him so effectually for his absence, that the painter had to give up seeing his other friends, and now went nowhere. Adelaide allowed the natural jealousy of women to be perceived when she heard that sometimes at eleven o'clock, on quitting the house, the painter still had visits to pay, and was to be seen in the most brilliant drawing-rooms of Paris. This mode of life, she assured him, was bad for his health; then, with the intense conviction to which the accent, the emphasis and the look of one we love lend so much weight, she asserted that a man who was obliged to expend his time and the charms of his wit on several women at once could not be the object of any very warm affection. Thus the painter was led, as much by the tyranny of his passion as by the exactions of a girl in love, to live exclusively in the little apartment where everything attracted him.

And never was there a purer or more ardent love. On both sides the same trustfulness, the same delicacy, gave their passion increase without the aid of those sacrifices by which many persons try to prove their affection. Between these two there was such a constant interchange of sweet emotion that they knew not which gave or received the most.

A spontaneous affinity made the union of their souls a close one. The progress of this true feeling was so rapid that two months after the accident to which the painter owed the happiness of knowing Adelaide, their lives were one life. From early morning the young girl, hearing footsteps overhead, could say to herself, "He is there." When Hippolyte went home to his mother at the dinner hour he never failed to look in on his neighbors, and in the evening he flew there at the accustomed hour with a lover's punctuality. Thus the most tyrannical woman or the most ambitious in the matter of love could not have found the smallest fault with the young painter. And Adelaide tasted of unmixed and unbounded happiness as she saw the fullest realization of the ideal of which, at her age, it is so natural to dream.

The old gentleman now came more rarely; Hippolyte, who had been jealous, had taken his place at the green table, and shared his constant ill-luck at cards. And sometimes, in the midst of his happiness, as he considered Madame de Rouville's disastrous position—for he had had more than one proof of her extreme poverty—an importunate thought would haunt him. Several times he had said to himself as he went home, "Strange! twenty francs every evening?" and he dared not confess to himself his odious suspicions.

He spent two months over the portrait, and when it was finished, varnished, and framed, he looked upon it as one of his best works. Madame la Baronne de Rouville had never spoken of it again. Was this from indifference or pride? The painter would not allow himself to account for this silence. He joyfully plotted with Adelaide to hang the picture in its place when Madame de Rouville should be out. So one day, during the walk her mother usually took in the Tuileries, Adelaide for the first time went up to Hippolyte's studio, on the pretext of seeing the portrait in the good light in which it had been painted. She stood speechless and motionless, but in ecstatic contemplation, in which all a woman's feelings were merged. For are they not all comprehended in boundless admiration for the man she loves? When the painter, uneasy at her silence, leaned forward to look at her, she held out her hand, unable to speak a word, but two tears fell from her eyes. Hippolyte took her hand and covered it with kisses; for a minute they looked at each other in silence, both longing to confess their love, and not daring. The painter kept her hand in his, and the same glow, the same throb, told them that their hearts were both beating wildly. The young girl, too greatly agitated, gently drew away from Hippolyte, and said, with a look of the utmost simplicity:

"You will make my mother very happy."

"What, only your mother?" he asked.

"Oh, I am too happy."

The painter bent his head and remained silent, frightened at the vehemence of the feelings which her tones stirred in his heart. Then, both understanding the perils of the situation, they went downstairs and hung up the picture in its place. Hippolyte dined for the first time with the Baroness, who, greatly overcome, and drowned in tears, must needs embrace him.

In the evening the old emigre, the Baron de Rouville's old comrade, paid the ladies a visit to announce that he had just been promoted to the rank of vice-admiral. His voyages by land over Germany and Russia had been counted as naval campaigns. On seeing the portrait he cordially shook the painter's hand, and exclaimed, "By Gad! though my old hulk does not deserve to be perpetuated, I would gladly give five hundred pistoles to see myself as like as that is to my dear old Rouville."

At this hint the Baroness looked at her young friend and smiled, while her face lighted up with an expression of sudden gratitude. Hippolyte suspected that the old admiral wished to offer him the price of both portraits while paying for his own. His pride as an artist, no less than his jealousy perhaps, took offence at the thought, and he replied:

"Monsieur, if I were a portrait-painter I should not have done this one."

The admiral bit his lip, and sat down to cards.

The painter remained near Adelaide, who proposed a dozen hands of piquet, to which he agreed. As he played he observed in Madame de Rouville an excitement over her game which surprised him. Never before had the old Baroness manifested so ardent a desire to win, or so keen a joy in fingering the old gentleman's gold pieces. During the evening evil suspicions troubled Hippolyte's happiness, and filled him with distrust. Could it be that Madame de Rouville lived by gambling? Was she playing at this moment to pay off some debt, or under the pressure of necessity? Perhaps she had not paid her rent. The old man seemed shrewd enough not to allow his money to be taken with impunity. What interest attracted him to this poverty-stricken house, he who was rich? Why, when he had formerly been so familiar with Adelaide, had he given up the rights he had acquired, and which were perhaps his due?

These involuntary reflections prompted him to watch the old man and the Baroness, whose meaning looks and certain sidelong glances cast at Adelaide displeased him. "Am I being duped?" was Hippolyte's last idea—horrible, scathing, for he believed it just enough to be tortured by it. He determined to stay after the departure of the two old men, to confirm or dissipate his suspicions. He drew out his purse to pay Adelaide; but carried away by his poignant thoughts, he laid it on the table, falling into a reverie of brief duration; then, ashamed of his silence, he rose, answered some commonplace question from Madame de Rouville, and went close up to her to examine the withered features while he was talking to her.

He went away, racked by a thousand doubts. He had gone down but a few steps when he turned back to fetch the forgotten purse.

"I left my purse here!" he said to the young girl.

"No," she said, reddening.

"I thought it was there," and he pointed to the card-table. Not finding it, in his shame for Adelaide and the Baroness, he looked at them with a blank amazement that made them laugh, turned pale, felt his waistcoat, and said, "I must have made a mistake. I have it somewhere no doubt."

In one end of the purse there were fifteen louis d'or, and in the other some small change. The theft was so flagrant, and denied with such effrontery, that Hippolyte no longer felt a doubt as to his neighbors' morals. He stood still on the stairs, and got down with some difficulty; his knees shook, he felt dizzy, he was in a cold sweat, he shivered, and found himself unable to walk, struggling, as he was, with the agonizing shock caused by the destruction of all his hopes. And at this moment he found lurking in his memory a number of observations, trifling in themselves, but which corroborated his frightful suspicions, and which, by proving the certainty of this last incident, opened his eyes as to the character and life of these two women.

Had they really waited till the portrait was given them before robbing him of his purse? In such a combination the theft was even more odious. The painter recollected that for the last two or three evenings Adelaide, while seeming to examine with a girl's curiosity the particular stitch of the worn silk netting, was probably counting the coins in the purse, while making some light jests, quite innocent in appearance, but no doubt with the object of watching for a moment when the sum was worth stealing.

"The old admiral has perhaps good reasons for not marrying Adelaide, and so the Baroness has tried — — "

But at this hypothesis he checked himself, not finishing his thought, which was contradicted by a very just reflection, "If the Baroness hopes to get me to marry her daughter," thought he, "they would not have robbed me."

Then, clinging to his illusions, to the love that already had taken such deep root, he tried to find a justification in some accident. "The purse must have fallen on the floor," said he to himself, "or I left it lying on my chair. Or perhaps I have it about me — I am so absent-minded!" He searched himself with hurried movements, but did not find the ill-starred purse. His memory cruelly retraced the fatal truth, minute by minute. He distinctly saw the purse lying on the green cloth; but then, doubtful no longer, he excused Adelaide, telling himself that persons in misfortune should not be so hastily condemned. There was, of course, some secret behind this apparently degrading action. He would not admit that that proud and noble face was a lie.

At the same time the wretched rooms rose before him, denuded of the poetry of love which beautifies everything; he saw them dirty and faded, regarding them as emblematic of an inner life devoid of honor, idle and vicious. Are not our feelings written, as it were, on the things about us?

Next morning he rose, not having slept. The heartache, that terrible malady of the soul, had made rapid inroads. To lose the bliss we dreamed of, to renounce our whole future, is a keener pang than that caused by the loss of known happiness, however complete it may have been; for is not Hope better than Memory? The thoughts into which our spirit is suddenly plunged are like a shoreless sea, in which we may swim for a moment, but where our love is doomed to drown and die. And it is a frightful death. Are not our feelings the most glorious part of our life? It is this partial death which, in certain delicate or powerful natures, leads to the terrible ruin produced by disenchantment, by hopes and passions betrayed. Thus it was with the young painter. He went out at a very early hour to walk under the fresh shade of the Tuileries, absorbed in his thoughts, forgetting everything in the world.

There by chance he met one of his most intimate friends, a school-fellow and studio-mate, with whom he had lived on better terms than with a brother.

"Why, Hippolyte, what ails you?" asked Francois Souchet, the young sculptor who had just won the first prize, and was soon to set out for Italy.

"I am most unhappy," replied Hippolyte gravely.

"Nothing but a love affair can cause you grief. Money, glory, respect — you lack nothing."

Insensibly the painter was led into confidences, and confessed his love. The moment he mentioned the Rue de Suresnes, and a young girl living on the fourth floor, "Stop, stop," cried Souchet lightly. "A little girl I see every morning at the Church of the Assumption, and with whom I have a flirtation. But, my dear fellow, we all know her. The mother is a Baroness. Do you really believe in a Baroness living up four flights of stairs? Brrr! Why, you are a relic of the golden age! We see the old mother here, in this avenue, every day; why, her face, her appearance, tell everything. What, have you not known her for what she is by the way she holds her bag?"

The two friends walked up and down for some time, and several young men who knew Souchet or Schinner joined them. The painter's adventure, which the sculptor regarded as unimportant, was repeated by him.

"So he, too, has seen that young lady!" said Souchet.

And then there were comments, laughter, innocent mockery, full of the liveliness familiar to artists, but which pained Hippolyte frightfully. A certain native reticence made him uncomfortable as he saw his heart's secret so carelessly handled, his passion rent, torn to tatters, a young and unknown girl, whose life seemed to be so modest, the victim of condemnation, right or wrong, but pronounced with such reckless indifference. He pretended to be moved by a spirit of contradiction, asking each for proofs of his assertions, and their jests began again.

"But, my dear boy, have you seen the Baroness' shawl?" asked Souchet.

"Have you ever followed the girl when she patters off to church in the morning?" said Joseph Bridau, a young dauber in Gros' studio.

"Oh, the mother has among other virtues a certain gray gown, which I regard as typical," said Bixiou, the caricaturist.

"Listen, Hippolyte," the sculptor went on. "Come here at about four o'clock, and just study the walk of both mother and daughter. If after that you still have doubts! well, no one can ever make anything of you; you would be capable of marrying your porter's daughter."

Torn by the most conflicting feelings, the painter parted from his friends. It seemed to him that Adelaide and her mother must be superior to these accusations, and at the bottom of his heart he was filled with remorse for having suspected the purity of this beautiful and simple girl. He went to his studio, passing the door of the rooms where Adelaide was, and conscious of a pain at his heart which no man can misapprehend. He loved Mademoiselle de Rouville so passionately that, in spite of the theft of the purse, he still worshiped her. His love was that of the Chevalier des Grieux admiring his mistress, and holding her as pure, even on the cart which carries such lost creatures to prison. "Why should not my love keep her the purest of women? Why abandon her to evil and to vice without holding out a rescuing hand to her?"

The idea of this mission pleased him. Love makes a gain of everything. Nothing tempts a young man more than to play the part of a good genius to a woman. There is something inexplicably romantic in such an enterprise which appeals to a highly-strung soul. Is it not the utmost stretch of devotion under the loftiest and most engaging aspect? Is there not something grand in the thought that we love enough still to love on when the love of others dwindles and dies?

Hippolyte sat down in his studio, gazed at his picture without doing anything to it, seeing the figures through tears that swelled in his eyes, holding his brush in his hand, going up to the canvas as if to soften down an effect, but not touching it. Night fell, and he was still in this attitude. Roused from his moodiness by the darkness, he went downstairs, met the old admiral on the way, looked darkly at him as he bowed, and fled.

He had intended going in to see the ladies, but the sight of Adelaide's protector froze his heart and dispelled his purpose. For the hundredth time he wondered what interest could bring this old prodigal, with his eighty thousand francs a year, to this fourth story, where he lost about forty francs every evening; and he thought he could guess what it was.

The next and following days Hippolyte threw himself into his work, and to try to conquer his passion by the swift rush of ideas and the ardor of composition. He half succeeded. Study consoled him, though it could not smother the memories of so many tender hours spent with Adelaide.

One evening, as he left his studio, he saw the door of the ladies' rooms half open. Somebody was standing in the recess of the window, and the position of the door and the staircase made it impossible that the painter should pass without seeing Adelaide. He bowed coldly, with a glance of supreme indifference; but judging of the girl's suffering by his own, he felt an inward shudder as he reflected on the bitterness which that look and that coldness must produce in a loving heart. To crown the most delightful feast which ever brought joy to two pure souls, by eight days of disdain, of the deepest and most utter contempt!—A frightful conclusion. And perhaps the purse had been found, perhaps Adelaide had looked for her friend every evening.

This simple and natural idea filled the lover with fresh remorse; he asked himself whether the proofs of attachment given him by the young girl, the delightful talks, full of the love that had so charmed him, did not deserve at least an inquiry; were not worthy of some justification. Ashamed of having resisted the promptings of his heart for a whole week, and feeling himself almost a criminal in this mental struggle, he called the same evening on Madame de Rouville.

All his suspicions, all his evil thoughts vanished at the sight of the young girl, who had grown pale and thin.

"Good heavens! what is the matter?" he asked her, after greeting the Baroness.

Adelaide made no reply, but she gave him a look of deep melancholy, a sad, dejected look, which pained him.

"You have, no doubt, been working hard," said the old lady. "You are altered. We are the cause of your seclusion. That portrait had delayed some pictures essential to your reputation."

Hippolyte was glad to find so good an excuse for his rudeness.

"Yes," he said, "I have been very busy, but I have been suffering—"

At these words Adelaide raised her head, looked at her lover, and her anxious eyes had now no hint of reproach.

"You must have thought us quite indifferent to any good or ill that may befall you?" said the old lady.

"I was wrong," he replied. "Still, there are forms of pain which we know not how to confide to any one, even to a friendship of older date than that with which you honor me."

"The sincerity and strength of friendship are not to be measured by time. I have seen old friends who had not a tear to bestow on misfortune," said the Baroness, nodding sadly.

"But you — what ails you?" the young man asked Adelaide.

"Oh, nothing," replied the Baroness. "Adelaide has sat up late for some nights to finish some little piece of woman's work, and would not listen to me when I told her that a day more or less did not matter — —"

Hippolyte was not listening. As he looked at these two noble, calm faces, he blushed for his suspicions, and ascribed the loss of his purse to some unknown accident.

This was a delicious evening to him, and perhaps to her too. There are some secrets which young souls understand so well. Adelaide could read Hippolyte's thoughts. Though he could not confess his misdeeds, the painter knew them, and he had come back to his mistress more in love, and more affectionate, trying thus to purchase her tacit forgiveness. Adelaide was enjoying such perfect, such sweet happiness, that she did not think she had paid too dear for it with all the grief that had so cruelly crushed her soul. And yet, this true concord of hearts, this understanding so full of magic charm, was disturbed by a little speech of Madame de Rouville's.

"Let us have our little game," she said, "for my old friend Kergarouet will not let me off."

These words revived all the young painter's fears; he colored as he looked at Adelaide's mother, but he saw nothing in her countenance but the expression of the frankest good-nature; no double meaning marred its charm; its keenness was not perifidious, its humor seemed kindly, and no trace of remorse disturbed its equanimity.

He sat down to the card-table. Adelaide took side with the painter, saying that he did not know piquet, and needed a partner.

All through the game Madame de Rouville and her daughter exchanged looks of intelligence, which alarmed Hippolyte all the more because he was winning; but at last a final hand left the lovers in the old lady's debt.

To feel for some money in his pocket the painter took his hands off the table, and he then saw before him a purse which Adelaide had slipped in front of him without his noticing it; the poor child had the old one in her hand, and, to keep her countenance, was looking into it for the money to pay her mother. The blood rushed to Hippolyte's heart with such force that he was near fainting.

The new purse, substituted for his own, and which contained his fifteen gold louis, was worked with gilt beads. The rings and tassels bore witness to Adelaide's good taste, and she had no doubt spent all her little hoard in ornamenting this pretty piece of work. It was impossible to say with greater delicacy that the painter's gift could only be repaid by some proof of affection.

Hippolyte, overcome with happiness, turned to look at Adelaide and her mother, and saw that they were tremulous with pleasure and delight at their little trick. He felt himself mean, sordid, a fool; he longed to punish himself, to rend his heart. A few tears rose to his eyes; by an irresistible impulse he sprang up, clasped Adelaide in his arms, pressed her to his heart, and stole a kiss; then with the simple heartiness of an artist, "I ask for her for my wife!" he exclaimed, looking at the Baroness.

Adelaide looked at him with half-wrathful eyes, and Madame de Rouville, somewhat astonished, was considering her reply, when the scene was interrupted by a ring at the bell. The old vice-admiral came in, followed by his shadow, and Madame Schinner. Having guessed the cause of the grief her son vainly endeavored to conceal, Hippolyte's mother had made inquiries among her friends concerning Adelaide. Very justly alarmed by the calumnies which weighed on the young girl, unknown to the Comte de Kergarouet, whose name she learned from the porter's wife, she went to report them to the vice-admiral; and he, in his rage, declared "he would crop all the scoundrels' ears for them."

Then, prompted by his wrath, he went on to explain to Madame Schinner the secret of his losing intentionally at cards, because the Baronne's pride left him none but these ingenious means of assisting her.

When Madame Schinner had paid her respects to Madame de Rouville, the Baroness looked at the Comte de Kergarouet, at the Chevalier du Halga—the friend of the departed Comtesse de Kergarouet—at Hippolyte, and Adelaide, and said, with the grace that comes from the heart, "So we are a family party this evening."

PARIS, May 1832

Milton Keynes UK
Ingram Content Group UK Ltd.
UKHW030856180424
441376UK00010B/281